Buster Posey

By Jon M. Fishman

AMAZING ATHLETES

Lerner Publications ◆ Minneapolis

Lerner Publications Company
A division of Lerner Publishing Group, Inc.
241 First Avenue North
Minneapolis, MN 55401 USA

For reading levels and more information, look up this title at www.lernerbooks.com.

Library of Congress Cataloging-in-Publication Data

Fishman, Jon M.
  Buster Posey / by Jon M. Fishman.
    pages cm. — (Amazing athletes)
  Includes bibliographical references and index.
  ISBN 978-1-4677-9384-1 (lb : alk. paper) — ISBN 978-1-4677-9617-0 (pb : alk. paper) —
ISBN 978-1-4677-9618-7 (eb pdf)
  1. Posey, Buster, 1987– —Juvenile literature. 2. Baseball players—United States—Biography—
Juvenile literature. I. Title.
GV865.P676F57 2016
796.357092—dc23 [B]   2015033974

Manufactured in the United States of America
1 – BP – 12/31/15

TABLE OF CONTENTS

Buster Posey winds up for a swing.

BASEBALL GIANT

San Francisco Giants **catcher** Buster Posey stood at home plate. His knees were bent, and his eyes were on the pitcher. He wiggled his bat and lifted his left leg. Buster let the ball zoom by. "Ball!" called the **umpire**.

Buster and the Giants were playing against the Texas Rangers on August 1, 2015. It was the seventh inning. Texas had the lead, 5–3. Buster was ready for the next pitch. He swung and sent the ball flying deep into the outfield. It sailed over the fence for a home run! Buster's blast made the score 5–4.

Buster runs the bases after hitting a home run against the Texas Rangers.

Buster came to bat again in the eighth inning with Texas ahead, 7–5. On the fifth pitch, Buster let loose with a mighty swing. *Smack!* He smashed the ball to the outfield for a **double**. Teammate Matt Duffy ran home to make the score 7–6. The Giants would score three more runs and win the game, 9–7.

Buster slides home to score a run against the Rangers.

The Giants celebrate their win over the Rangers.

The Giants have been one of Major League Baseball's most successful teams in recent years. They beat the Rangers in 2010 to win the World Series. Then they won the World Series in 2012 and again in 2014. Buster was the team's catcher for all three championships.

Buster has enjoyed incredible success in Major League Baseball. But his path to stardom hasn't been easy. As a boy growing up in Georgia, he learned that hard work is the best way to achieve your dreams. That lesson helped Buster overcome a serious injury that could have ended his career. The injury taught him to enjoy every moment of the sport he loves. "I've seen that it can be taken away quick," he said.

Buster catches the ball during a game in 2015.

Buster grew up in Leesburg, Georgia.

FAMILY SPORT

Buster Posey was born on March 27, 1987, in Leesburg, Georgia. His full name is Gerald Dempsey Posey III. He shares a name with his father and grandfather. Buster's father goes by Demp. But when Demp was a child, his grandmother called him Buster. When Demp had his first child, he started calling the boy Buster right away. The name stuck.

Buster's mom, Traci, and dad, Demp, encouraged their children's love of baseball.

Buster has two younger brothers named Jess and Jack and a younger sister named Sam. The four children loved to play baseball. They even played inside. Sam practiced pitching by throwing at a pillow in her bedroom. One day she missed the pillow and put a dent in the wall. Buster practiced **sliding** in the family's living room. He slid too hard and put a hole in the wall with his foot.

Demp and his wife, Traci, decided they had to do something to keep their children from destroying the house. They set up a **batting cage** in the family's huge backyard. Demp pitched to the kids while Traci ran down fly balls. Friends from all around the neighborhood came to the Poseys' backyard to play ball.

Buster isn't the only famous person from Leesburg. It's also the hometown of country music star Luke Bryan.

Buster spent plenty of time on the baseball diamond in Leesburg.

11

In 2002, Buster began attending Lee County High School (LCHS). He pitched and played **shortstop** for the school's baseball team. Buster had a lot of natural talent. But it was his hard work that really stood out. Rob Williams coached Buster at LCHS. "Most kids want to practice the things that they already do well,"

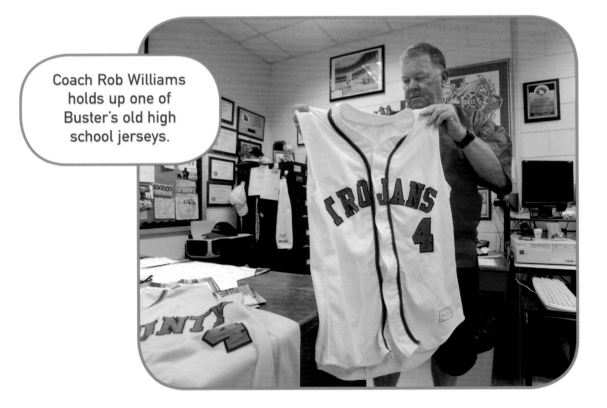

Coach Rob Williams holds up one of Buster's old high school jerseys.

Williams said. "The difference with Buster is that he wanted to work on the things that aren't as much fun."

By 2004, Buster's will to work hard made him the star of the team. He set a school record

Buster worked hard to improve his game in high school.

with a .544 **batting average** for the season. He also set records for most **runs batted in (RBIs)** with 46 and most hits with 56. As a pitcher, Buster won 10 games and lost only one all year.

Buster *(second row, second from left)* poses with his brother Jack *(second row, third from left)* in this 2005 high school baseball team photo.

CATCHING UP

As a high school senior in 2005, Buster continued to prove he was one of the best young baseball players in Georgia. He set an LCHS record with 14 home runs for the year. He also had a perfect record of 12–0 as a pitcher.

Buster wanted to keep playing baseball after high school. He was one of the top-rated players his age in the country, so he had a lot of options. He decided to attend Florida State University (FSU). The Florida State Seminoles had a winning baseball team. And the school wasn't too far from Buster's home in Georgia.

In 2006, Buster did well with the Seminoles. Even though he was just a freshman, he played shortstop in every game of the season. His .346 batting average and 85 hits were both second best on the team.

Buster *(left)* tags out a player trying to steal second base during a Seminoles game in 2006.

Before the start of the next season, FSU coaches went to Buster with an unusual idea. They wanted to know what he thought about switching positions and becoming a catcher. Catchers are a big part of almost every play during a baseball game. A catcher must have strong leadership skills, and the coaches saw those skills in Buster. They also knew Buster had the strength and talent to handle the tough position.

Buster *(left)* became the Seminoles' catcher in his second college season.

Buster agreed to the switch. He had never played catcher before and had a lot to learn. "The first two days, I had to teach him to put his gear on," said FSU coach Mike Martin Jr. "Three weeks later, it was, 'Holy cow, this guy's going to be really good.'"

Buster once played all nine fielding positions in a single game with Florida State. He also hit a **grand slam** during the game.

Buster *(left)* learned quickly and became a great catcher.

In 2007, Buster once again played every game for the Seminoles. But this season he played catcher. Even though he had just taken up the position, his defense was solid. And the change didn't hurt his batting skills. He led FSU with 66 RBIs. His .382 batting average was fifth best in the **conference**.

Buster hits a home run for Florida State.

During his final season at FSU, Buster was one of the top players in college baseball.

BUSTING OUT

Buster's next season was his greatest yet. By June 3, 2008, he was batting .468 with 86 RBIs. Those were the top marks in **Division I** college baseball. He had also launched 24 home runs, which was fourth best.

On June 5, Major League Baseball held its yearly **draft**. The Giants had the fifth overall pick, and they chose Buster. The young catcher had never been to San Francisco, but he was ready to work hard for his new team. "Hopefully, I can be an impact player for the San Francisco Giants," he said.

Buster began his pro career in the **minor leagues**. In 2009, he played 115 minor-league games and notched a .325 batting average. He also smacked 18 home runs. The Giants called him up to play for the major-league team. But in seven games, Buster had just two hits.

He began the 2010 season back in the minor leagues. But on May 29, he was again called up to play with the Giants. This time, he made the impact he was hoping for. In his first game, Buster came to bat with San Francisco ahead,

1–0. He blasted a **line drive** to knock in a run. In the fifth inning, he smacked another hit and another RBI. Then he did it again in his final at bat of the game. The Giants crushed the Arizona Diamondbacks, 12–1.

Buster smashes a hit in his first game with the Giants in 2010.

Buster holds his first World Series championship trophy.

The Giants had been in third place in their **division** when they called Buster up from the minor leagues. But with their new star leading the way, San Francisco began climbing the standings. They made it to the **playoffs** and kept on winning. Then, on November 1, 2010, the Giants beat the Texas Rangers to win the World Series!

Two weeks later, Buster was named 2010 **Rookie** of the Year for the **National League**. His 18 home runs and .305 batting average for the season were impressive. But he sealed the award by helping the Giants win the championship.

In 2011, Buster's sister, Sam, began playing college softball for Valdosta State. "I still think Sam is the most athletic of [my children]," Demp said. "Buster, I think he's just the hardest worker."

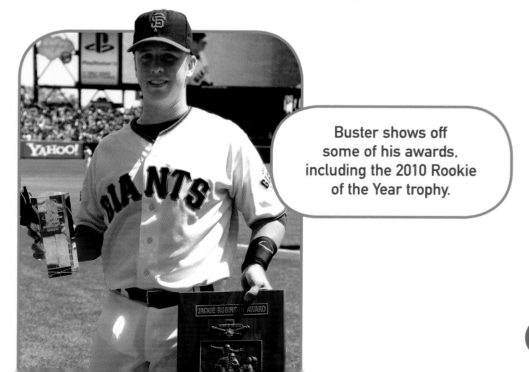

Buster shows off some of his awards, including the 2010 Rookie of the Year trophy.

Buster suits up to catch against the Florida Marlins in 2011.

PAIN BEFORE GLORY

Buster and his teammates had high hopes for the 2011 season. By May 25, the Giants led their division. That night, they played against the Florida Marlins in San Francisco. With the score tied 6–6 in the 12th inning, a Marlins player hit a high fly ball to the outfield. Florida's Scott Cousins came racing home from third base.

The Giants threw the ball toward home plate. Buster tried to block the plate, but Cousins smashed into him. The ball rolled away as Buster slammed into the ground. He slapped the field in pain. He dug his fingers into the dirt and clenched his teeth. Buster had a broken bone in his lower left leg.

Buster (right) breaks his leg during a crash at home plate.

The crowd was stunned. They chanted "Posey! Posey!" as Buster was helped off the field. He wouldn't play baseball again in 2011. Without their star catcher, the Giants fell out of first place and missed the playoffs.

On August 15, 2011, Buster's wife, Kristen, gave birth to twins. Their names are Lee Dempsey and Addison Lynn.

Buster gets help leaving the field after breaking his leg.

Buster healed and went to **rehab**. It was a long and painful process. But he had always worked hard, even when the work wasn't fun. Buster returned to the field for the beginning

Buster gears up for spring training in 2012.

of the 2012 season. He quickly proved that the broken leg was behind him. He batted .336 for the year and bashed 24 home runs.

The Giants won their division. Then they won game after game in the playoffs. They made it all the way to the World Series against the Detroit Tigers. The Giants won the first three games of the series. In Game 4, Buster hit a two-run home run to help San Francisco **sweep** the Tigers. The Giants were world champs!

In 2014, the Giants reached the World Series again. This time, they took seven games to beat the Kansas City Royals. Buster had three hits in the final game. San Francisco had won the World Series three times in five years since Buster joined the team! "I mean, it's unbelievable," he said. With Buster behind the plate, the Giants are one of the best teams in baseball.

The Giants celebrate their World Series win over Kansas City.

Selected Career Highlights

2015 Voted to the Major League Baseball All-Star Game for the third time

2014 Helped Giants win the World Series

2013 Voted to the Major League Baseball All-Star Game for the second time

2012 Voted to the Major League Baseball All-Star Game for the first time
Won the batting title with the highest batting average in the National League
Won the Comeback Player of the Year Award
Helped Giants win the World Series
Voted National League Most Valuable Player

2011 Missed most of the season with a broken leg

2010 Helped Giants win the World Series
Voted National League Rookie of the Year

2009 Played first Major League Baseball games

2008 Led all Division I college players with a .468 batting average and 86 RBIs
Drafted by the Giants with the fifth overall pick in the draft

2007 Switched positions and became a catcher for Florida State

2006 Was the starting shortstop for Florida State as a freshman

2005 Starred as a batter and a pitcher for Lee County High School

Glossary

batting average: a number that describes how often a baseball player gets a hit

batting cage: screens set up around home plate to catch balls during batting practice

catcher: the player behind home plate who catches throws from the pitcher

conference: a group of college teams that play against one another

division: a group of teams that play against one another. The National League has three divisions.

Division I: the top level of college sports

double: a hit that allows a player to reach second base

draft: a yearly event in which Major League Baseball teams select high school and college players

grand slam: a home run hit with a player on every base

line drive: a ball that flies in a straight line not far from the ground

minor leagues: a series of teams in which players gain experience and improve their skills before going to the major leagues

National League: one of Major League Baseball's two leagues. The National League has 15 teams, including the San Francisco Giants.

playoffs: a series of games held to decide a champion

rehab: an exercise program used to heal injuries

rookie: a first-year player

runs batted in (RBIs): the number of runners able to score on a hitter's at bat

shortstop: a player who takes the position in the field between second base and third base

sliding: diving headfirst or feetfirst into a base

sweep: to win all the games in a series

umpire: a person who watches a baseball game to make sure the rules are being followed

Further Reading & Websites

Braun, Eric. *Super Baseball Infographics*. Minneapolis: Lerner Publications, 2015.

Kennedy, Mike, and Mark Stewart. *Long Ball: The Legend and Lore of the Home Run*. Minneapolis: Millbrook Press, 2006.

Patrick, Jean L. S. *The Baseball Adventure of Jackie Mitchell, Girl Pitcher vs. Babe Ruth*. Minneapolis: Graphic Universe, 2011.

The Official Site of Major League Baseball
http://www.mlb.com/home
Major League Baseball's official website provides fans with the latest scores and game schedules as well as information on players, teams, and baseball history.

The Official Site of the San Francisco Giants
http://sanfrancisco.giants.mlb.com/index.jsp?c_id=sf
The San Francisco Giants' official site includes the team schedule and game results. Visitors can also find late-breaking news, biographies of Buster Posey and other players and coaches, and much more.

Sports Illustrated Kids
http://www.sikids.com
The *Sports Illustrated Kids* website covers all sports, including baseball.

Index

Photo Acknowledgments

The images in this book are used with the permission of: © Albert Pena/ZUMA Press/Corbis, p. 4; © Rick Yeatts/Getty Images, p. 5; AP Photo/LM Otero, p. 6; © Rick Yeatts/Getty Images, p. 7; © Jason O. Watson/Getty Images, p. 8; © Zuma Press, Inc./Alamy, p. 9; © Brad Mangin/MLB Photos/Getty Images, p. 10; © Erik Lesser/ZUMA Press, Inc/Alamy, p. 11; © Erik S. Lesser/Alamy, pp. 12, 14; Seth Poppel Yearbook Library, p. 13; AP Photo/Alan Diaz, p. 15; AP Photo/Steve Cannon, pp. 16, 18; AP Photo/Phil Coale, p. 17; Cliff Welch/Icon SMI/Newscom, p. 19; © Ezra Shaw/Getty Images, pp. 21, 24; © Ronald Martinez/Getty Images, p. 22; © Brad Mangin/MLB Photos/Getty Images, p. 23; AP Photo/Marcio Jose Sanchez, pp. 25, 26, 27; AP Photo/Charlie Niebergall, p. 28; © Dilip Vishwanat/Getty Images, p. 29.

Front cover: © Brad Mangin/MLB Photos/Getty Images.

Main body text set in Caecilia LT Std 55 Roman 16/28.
Typeface provided by Adobe Systems.